D0346229

For Steve, my humble
waste warrior – W.S.

For Aunt Rita, who sparked
my love for nature – P.D.

Text © 2021 Wenda Shurety, Illustrations © 2021 Paddy Donnelly

First published in 2021 by Storyhouse Publishing
3 Malvern Villas, Bath BA1 5JS, United Kingdom · www.storyhousepublishing.com

ISBN 9781916281837

Designed by Ali Halliday

Printed in Heshan, Guangdong, China by Leo Paper Products

3% from the cover price of each book sold goes to the Marine Conservation Society,
a UK marine charity with a vision of seas full of life · www.mcsuk.org
Registered charity no. 1004005 (England & Wales); SC037480 (Scotland).

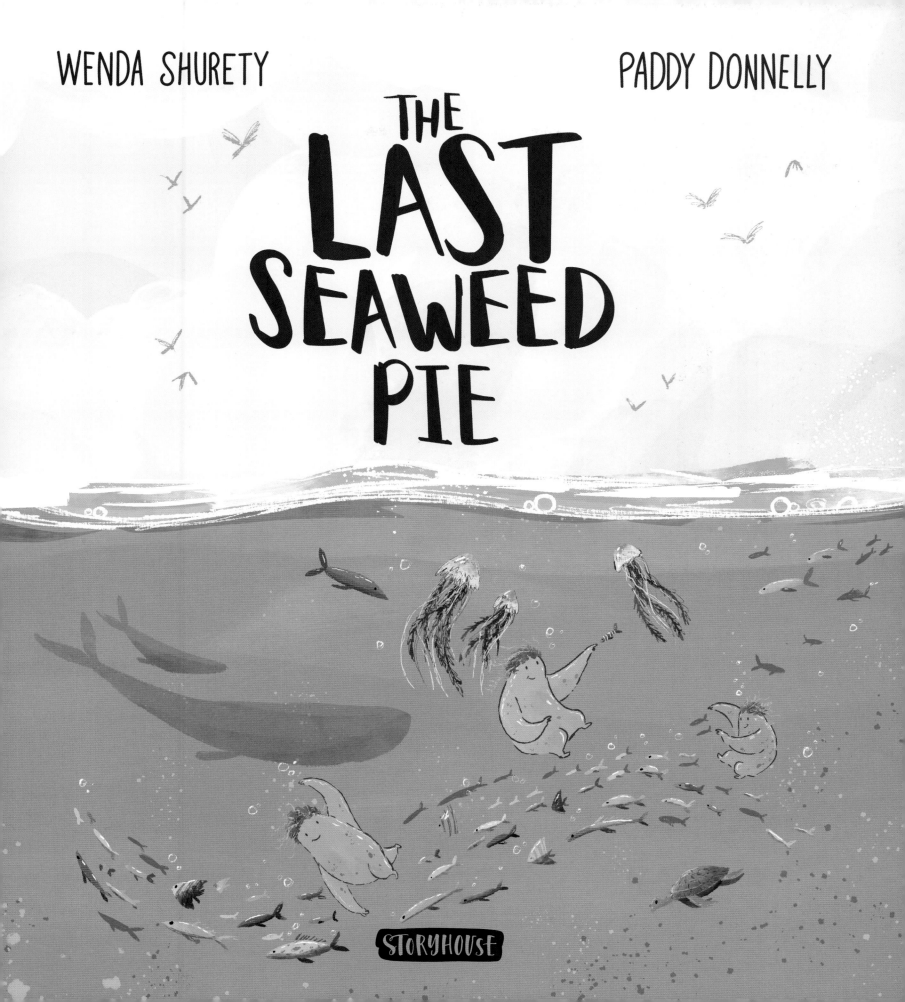

WENDA SHURETY

PADDY DONNELLY

THE LAST SEAWEED PIE

STORYHOUSE

The Treeple lived up high in the trees.
They liked to build houses of sticks,
climb with the lemurs
and bake papaya pies.

But most of all,
the Treeple loved to
make things.

The Seaple lived deep down in the ocean.
They liked to build houses of shells,
swim with the fishes
and bake seaweed pie.

But most of all, the Seaple
loved to *watch nature*.

Up in the canopy,
the Treeple would
make *and* **mould**,

sew *and* **saw**

and **bang** *and* **tap**.

The **more** things they created,
the **more** they wanted.

When something new was made,
they threw away the old things, broken or not.

Soon, there was no space on the branches
for all the Treeple, the new things and the old things.

"To make room,
we'll move the old things
to the **ground**,"
said the Treeple.

The Treeple returned to their
making *and* moulding,
sewing *and* sawing *and*
banging *and* tapping.

Soon, there
was no space
on the ground.

"To make room, we'll move
the old things to the ocean,"
said the Treeple.

Up in the canopy, the sounds
of creation continued to echo
through the forest.

Meanwhile, deep in the ocean, the Seaple gazed up
at the dark shapes floating above.

"Oh look,
that shape looks like a
seahorse."

"Is that an octopus?"

"Wow, that shape is as big as a whale!"

But as the shapes grew in size,
    life down in the ocean became gloomier.

One day, a big dark blob hovered above and
blocked out the light.

Fish became caught up in the mass of old things.
Sea creatures and plants began to disappear.

After eating the **last** seaweed pie,
the Seaple decided it was time to leave.

With heavy hearts, they set out
to find a new place to live.

When they reached the shore,
they saw different looking
creatures living in the trees.

With joy, they climbed up to meet them.

The Treeple shook their heads.

"We are the Treeple and
there is **no** room
for you here."

The Seaple looked down
at the ground and out to sea.

"But we have **nowhere** to go,"
they pleaded.

A young Treeple stepped forward
and took a deep breath.

"Maybe if we stopped
making things,
we would have room
for the Seaple."

The Treeple frowned. "Stopped **making** things?
But that's what we do!"

A Seaple picked up an old pot to be thrown away.
"You could make a great **pie dish** with this."

The Treeple looked around at the piles of old things,
then all spoke at once.

"I could make some
chairs out of this table!"

"I could make a
hat out of this coat!"

"I could make a bed out of this box!"

As old things were
made into new things,
the trees, the ground
and the sea began
to clear.

Eventually, the Seaple could return
to their home in the ocean.

The Treeple and the Seaple
became great friends,
and some Seaple remained to show
the Treeple about the wonder of nature . . .

and swap **pie** recipes.

Be an Ocean Hero!

You can help the Seaple and their underwater friends so that they can live safely and happily. Even if you live a long way from the coast, the plastic you throw away could make its way into the sea.

Litter dropped on the street doesn't stay there. Rainwater and wind carries the light plastic into streams and rivers, and through drains. Drains lead to the ocean!

Here are some things that you and your family can do to help . . .

Use Less Plastic. Small changes make a big difference. Swap to reuseable water bottles, create green party bags with paper notebooks and flower seeds and pack an eco-friendly lunch box with reusable containers and plenty of fruit which doesn't have plastic packaging.

Shop Wisely and Recycle. Buy things that can be recycled and take reusable bags to the shops. Mend or gift old toys and clothes instead of throwing them away.

Help Clean Up. Go litter picking! With a parent or carer, help keep the natural world clean by picking up rubbish. But be careful – always wear protective gloves and never grab anything that looks sharp or dangerous.

Look After the Planet. Carbon dioxide is bad for our oceans, so walk or ride your bike instead of travelling by car.

Save Water. Turn water off when you brush your teeth. Take shorter showers and shallower baths to help reduce the amount of water you use.

Keep Learning. Read books, visit aquariums and ask your teacher or carer about oceans. Knowledge is power!

Visit the Marine Conservation Society at **www.mcsuk.org** *for more ideas of ways to help.*